Agatha
Girl of Mystery

GROSSET & DUNLAP
Penguin Young Readers Group
An Imprint of Penguin Random House LLC

Original Title: *Agatha Mistery: Crociera con Delitto*
Text by Sir Steve Stevenson
Original cover and illustrations by Stefano Turconi

English language edition copyright © 2016 Penguin Random House LLC. Original edition published by Istituto Geografico De Agostini S.p.A., Italy, 2012 © 2012 Atlantyca Dreamfarm s.r.l., Italy

International Rights © Atlantyca S.p.A.–via Leopardi 8, 20123 Milano, Italia
foreignrights@atlantyca.it–www.atlantyca.com

Published in 2016 by Grosset & Dunlap, an imprint of Penguin Random House LLC, 345 Hudson Street, New York, New York 10014. GROSSET & DUNLAP is a trademark of Penguin Random House LLC. Printed in the USA.

Library of Congress Cataloging-in-Publication Data is available.

10 9 8 7 6 5 4 3 2 1

ISBN 978-0-448-48681-9

Agatha

Girl of Mystery

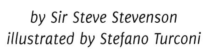

The Crime on the Norwegian Sea

by Sir Steve Stevenson
illustrated by Stefano Turconi

translated by Siobhan Tracey
adapted by Maya Gold

Grosset & Dunlap
An Imprint of Penguin Random House

TENTH MISSION
Agents

Agatha
Twelve years old, an aspiring mystery writer; has a formidable memory

Dash
Agatha's cousin and student at the private school Eye International Detective Academy

Chandler
Butler and former boxer with impeccable British style

Watson
Obnoxious Siberian cat with the nose of a bloodhound

Edgar Allan Mistery
Dash's superathletic dad, who never misses a chance to compete with his son

DESTINATION

The Norwegian fjords

OBJECTIVE

Capture the top secret-document
thief who murdered a notorious spy,
before the luxury cruise ship *King Arthur*
reaches its next destination!

The Investigation Begins...

$\mathcal{D}$ashiell Mistery was a lanky fourteen-year-old boy with the muscle tone of wet spaghetti. His long black hair always looked as if he'd just rolled out of bed, or off the couch where he often spent all morning sleeping. He stayed up till all hours every night tinkering with all the amazing high-tech devices in his penthouse on the top floor of London's Baker Palace. His friends had nicknamed Dash "Doctor Jekyll" because of his night-owl habits, which reminded them of a mad scientist locked away in his lab.

When he first heard the nickname, Dash laughed and tried to shrug it off. But there was

no way to deny that everyone in the Mistery family was a little . . . well, odd. They were deeply eccentric people with unusual jobs, living in every corner of the globe. Dash had an unusual job of his own, which he kept well-hidden from almost everyone. With a few rare exceptions, nobody knew about his stunning success as a teenage detective!

Even his father, Edgar Allan Mistery, knew nothing about all the dangerous missions that Eye International Detective School had assigned to Dash, investigating thefts, kidnappings, and other crimes. Edgar had divorced Dash's mother a long time ago and remarried recently. When his ex-wife enrolled their son at the prestigious academy, Edgar had made Dash promise to study hard and ace all his tests so that someday he'd be the director of London's famous Scotland Yard. Then Edgar had burst out laughing, always a sign he was throwing down some kind of

challenge. A former Olympic athlete, he was a very competitive man, and nothing made him as happy as winning.

Ever since then, Dash had struggled to do his best in his classes and on every investigation to which he was assigned. But not this week—he was about to go on a vacation! No high-pressure final exams, no unsolved mysteries lurking on the horizon. The aspiring detective had seven whole days of blissful relaxation ahead. There was only one hitch: He'd be spending this otherwise perfect week with his dad.

"Same old story whenever I see him," Dash grumbled, climbing the ladder to the high diving board. When he got to the top, he grabbed hold of both rails. The turquoise pool shimmered on Deck Twelve of the majestic ocean liner *King Arthur* as it plowed through tall waves off the Norwegian coast. Wherever he looked, the young detective saw water: the endless, foaming sea,

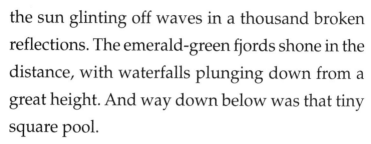

the sun glinting off waves in a thousand broken reflections. The emerald-green fjords shone in the distance, with waterfalls plunging down from a great height. And way down below was that tiny square pool.

"What are you waiting for, Dash?" his father yelled from the side of the pool where he stood with his video camera, ready to shoot yet another video clip of his son doing something he hated.

Tanned, fit, and boyish, Edgar still looked like the top athlete he'd been.

"Are you planning to lose every challenge?" he said with a mocking laugh. "I already beat you at swimming and holding your breath underwater. You're such a wimp!"

Dash gritted his teeth as he inched forward on the wobbly diving board. Why had he ever agreed to go on this cruise with his dad? He knew it would be unbearable.

Sun, fun, and endless free food, he reminded himself.

The best way to settle this once and for all was to prove to his father he wasn't a loser. So Dash took a deep breath, trying to fight back his fear of heights, and stepped to the edge of the diving board.

"Let's see what you've got!" Edgar Mistery said with a cackle. "Did you see what a big splash I made with my double back somersault? Try and beat *that*, if you can!"

"Yeah, right . . . This time I'll show you,"

Dash muttered without much conviction. He set his feet carefully at the edge and spread his arms wide for what he hoped would look like a magnificent swan dive. "I'm . . . um . . . almost ready!"

But something distracted him.

A crowd of onlookers stood next to the pool, cheering and catcalling. The only person missing was his father's new wife, Olympic speed skating champion Kristi Linstrid. She sat under a large umbrella slathering sunscreen on little Ilse, the latest addition to the Mistery family. Dash's baby sister shared his blue eyes, his long legs—and his obsession with shiny high-tech devices. She had spotted his EyeNet in his unzipped sports bag, and was fooling around with its buttons.

"Oh no!" mumbled Dash. "If she turns it on, I'll be in big trouble. Good thing I encrypted the passcode."

The shiny prototype, designed to look like a

trendy cell phone, was only available to students of Eye International. Hidden inside the EyeNet's titanium shell was a high-powered hard drive with a wealth of secret archives, online databases, and state-of-the-art apps to assist with investigations.

"Go, Dash! You rock!" cheered a group of teen girls on the edge of the pool. He peered down and blushed beet red as they waved and blew kisses at him.

"What a heartbreaker!" Edgar Mistery declared proudly. He turned to the noisy group of bikini-clad fans. "We're throwing a party for my son tonight. Want to come?"

The girls squealed happily, as though they'd been invited to a private party with a rock star.

Embarrassed, Dash covered his face with his hands. It was official: This was the most awkward vacation ever. All he'd wanted was to spend a few days away from his boring homework routine, and he'd bent over backward to get permission from his school . . . for *this*?

Tormented by these thoughts, Dash thought about giving up on Edgar's challenge. He could climb back down the ladder, join Kristi and Ilse, and stretch out on a deck chair, relaxing in peace. As he turned his gaze toward them, a scene unfolded as if in slow motion.

This is what he saw. The EyeNet started screeching and blinking like crazy, and little Ilse freaked out and flung it away. It flew through the air, clattering over the slippery tiles and sliding toward the pool.

Dash had been assigned a new mission, and his EyeNet was about to drown!

Without stopping to think, Dash launched himself off the diving board with a spectacular twist. He plunged into the water with perfect style and popped up the edge, resurfacing just in time to grab the EyeNet a second before it hit the water.

"Got it!" Dash gasped.

He turned it on to make sure it was still working. It was. He was so relieved that he didn't notice that everyone was gaping at him with their jaws dropped, amazed by his champion dive. The girls broke into cheers, but Dash had already shot out of the pool, grabbed his T-shirt and flip-flops, and charged off to find his cousin Agatha in the ship's library. He ran past the lifeguard and into the hall, dripping water all over the carpet, ignoring every one of the ship's many rules. He pressed the elevator button, his eyes never leaving the EyeNet's screen.

The message from Eye International wasted no words. He reread it twenty times:

AGENT DM14,

MANHUNT ON THE *KING ARTHUR*. CODE NAME: "OPERATION BISMARCK." DETAILS IN ATTACHED FILE. PROCEED WITH UTMOST URGENCY.

PS: SORRY TO WRECK YOUR VACATION!

The elevator doors opened, and Dash pushed in between the stunned passengers. Wreck his vacation? Not in the least! The boy breathed a sigh of relief. An investigation was the perfect way to escape from his dad.

Library at Sea

*A*spiring writer Agatha Mistery had memorized every inch of the *King Arthur*. When the towering ship had first launched from the docks of Southampton a few years before, there had been hundreds of newspaper articles and television programs describing its elegant British design and state-of-the-art navigation systems.

Bigger than the *Titanic*, and powered by massive turbine engines, the *King Arthur* carried five thousand passengers and crew members on cruises all over the world. It boasted all the usual tourist attractions, distributed over its sixteen decks: restaurants, movie theaters, swimming

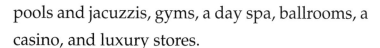

pools and jacuzzis, gyms, a day spa, ballrooms, a casino, and luxury stores.

But Agatha had no interest in any of these entertainments. Wearing a classic beribboned white hat and a cool linen dress, she sat scribbling notes into her trusty notebook. From the moment they set sail, she had been happily lost among the rare maritime books and ancient maps in the ship's library on Deck Six, a quiet place organized in the best Oxford tradition.

What a gold mine for mystery stories! Her imagination ran wild.

"What do you think about a dark creature from the abyss coming up to the surface to menace our heroes?" she whispered to Chandler. She was plotting a mystery novel set on a cruise ship lost in the icy waters of the Arctic Circle.

The smart, pretty twelve-year-old often found inspiration in the far-flung places she and Dash got to visit. Sailing along the Norwegian fjords evoked images of stark contrast: the striking beauty of the picturesque landscape and the terror of the high seas. She pointed to a dramatic painting of a giant tentacled creature, framed on the library's wall.

"They might think their ship has been seized by the legendary kraken," she went on, tapping the tip of her small upturned nose.

Chandler approached the painting and bent

his enormous ex-heavyweight frame to examine it closer. "Did you just say *kraken*, Miss Agatha?" he asked. "The giant squid from the Viking sagas?" Without waiting for her to answer, he rubbed his square jaw and observed, "It might seem a little implausible."

A brilliant smile lit the girl's face. "It's a 'red herring,' a plot device to raise the tension," she said with a nod. "Of course the kraken won't ever show up. It only exists in the characters' imaginations."

"Um, yes . . . well, of course." Chandler coughed.

The Mistery House butler and jack-of-all-trades adjusted his tie and petted Watson, who sat on his shoulders. Every so often, the white Siberian cat raised his nose and immediately dropped it back down, mewing in protest. The ship was kept sparkling clean, and the scent of disinfectant bothered his sensitive nose.

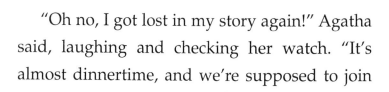

"Oh no, I got lost in my story again!" Agatha said, laughing and checking her watch. "It's almost dinnertime, and we're supposed to join Uncle Edgar tonight at the welcome dinner."

Dash's dad was the brother of Agatha's own father, Arthur Mistery. Along with his love of competitive sports, Edgar was fluent in dozens of languages. Always ready to change careers at the drop of a hat, he was just as impatient with marriage and had recently tied the knot for the third time. He had three children, one from each marriage. The oldest son was the Parisian painter Gaston, followed by Dash, and now Ilse. Edgar, Kristi, and Ilse had boarded that morning at the Norwegian port of Bergen, joining Agatha, Dash, and Chandler, who had set sail from England the previous day.

"If you don't mind, Miss," Chandler said gallantly. "Let me carry your books."

"It's a pretty big pile," she admitted, eyeing

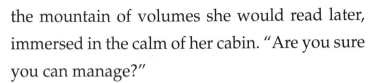

the mountain of volumes she would read later, immersed in the calm of her cabin. "Are you sure you can manage?"

"No problem," declared the butler.

He picked them all up in one strong arm, while Watson reached down to swipe at a rolled-up map. Chandler gently moved it away and was about to leave the library when a great commotion broke out at the door.

"Stop right there, sir!" somebody yelled.

"You're dripping water all over!" another voice shouted.

A tall, lanky boy, drenched from head to toe, was being chased by two uniformed stewards.

"Arrrrrgh!" cried Dash, dodging first one, then another clumsy attempt to tackle him. "I have to speak with my cousin . . . GAAAH!"

He crashed into Chandler. Books scattered all over the carpet, the Siberian cat's back arched, and Chandler went down with a tremendous *thump*.

Dash found himself sprawled across the butler's stomach, astonished that he'd knocked the former champ onto the carpet.

"Did I hurt you?" asked Dash, momentarily shaken. Then his eyes narrowed and he blurted as if nothing had happened, "Agatha! Where is she? I need her!"

"Right behind you, dear cousin," said Agatha, sounding reproachful. She was staring at him with her arms folded.

"It's just . . . you see, I got a . . . ," Dash tried to explain, but a stern look from Agatha stopped him in mid-sentence.

"Is your poor mother still running a fever?" Agatha improvised, feigning concern. "Summer flus can be brutal, especially in London's humidity. Let's go ask the ship's doctor for his advice. Come with me!"

Hearing her words, the stewards calmed down. They walked away, grumbling that

even when someone was sick, rules should be respected. Agatha's ruse had worked. Since Dash was still dripping wet, the group left the library and entered the hall, which was filled with passengers from all over the world.

As soon as they found a secluded nook, Agatha took control. "Spit it out, Dash," she urged. "What sort of mission have you been given?"

"H-how did you know I'm on a mission?" Her cousin was stunned.

Chandler responded first. "No offense, Master Dash, but whenever you choke your EyeNet in your fist like that, it's a classic sign there's a red alert."

"Exactly." Agatha nodded. "But get to the point. What can you possibly do? We'll be at sea all night, sailing from Bergen to Trondheim. We won't be able to leave the *King Arthur* till dawn. Not to mention we're with Uncle Edgar . . ."

"Dad can't get involved!" Dash blurted. "If he knew about my investigations, he'd try to take over!" Frowning, he checked to make sure there was no one nearby, then clicked on his EyeNet and showed them the message. "There's no need to leave," he said smugly. "The manhunt will take place on board the *King Arthur*!"

Chandler raised an eyebrow in surprise, while Watson peered down from his shoulder, his ears pricked.

"'Operation Bismarck' is a strange name," mused Agatha, peering at the screen. "If my memory serves me correctly, Otto von Bismarck was a great Prussian leader in the nineteenth century. He unified Germany and was the nation's first chancellor."

"Is that so?" asked the butler, smoothing his hair. "I've wondered about the origins of eggs Bismarck for years." Agatha's parents were often away on business trips, so he had

become an accomplished chef.

"You can throw out the keys to your memory drawers this time, cousin." Dash smirked like a know-it-all. "*Bismarck* is the code name of a famous spy!"

"How do you know that?" asked Agatha.

Dash chuckled. "I just read the file!"

"What else did it say?" she pressed.

Dash shook his head. "Um, well . . . I only gave it a quick glance . . . I'll need to connect the EyeNet to my laptop to access the rest."

Agatha turned toward the elevators, and the others followed. "I bet our spy is a German in his sixties," she said. "Code names are rarely as random as people think."

"Is that just a guess?" asked Dash, hurrying to keep up.

"Not at all," she said calmly. "You'll see, I'll be right."

Moments later, they reached Dash's cabin on

Deck Eight. It was so messy, it looked as if it had been hit by a typhoon. He dug out his laptop from between rumpled bedsheets and checked the files he had downloaded.

It didn't take long to find out that, as usual, Agatha's theory was correct.

Dinner with a Spy

*T*he *King Arthur* was wending its way up the jagged seacoast of Norway. After a stop at Trondheim Fjord, the ship would cross the Arctic Circle and sail to North Cape on Magerøya island, where the passengers would witness a truly unique phenomenon: the midnight sun. During the summer months, the sun set very late and only dipped below the horizon for a few hours. The brief arctic nights were clear and bright, going from dusk to dawn without ever getting completely dark.

But the three Londoners had other things on their minds.

"Can you replay Agent AP36's message again?" asked Agatha, biting her lip. "I'm confused by one detail."

Dash pressed a button. A man with craggy features and a sprinkling of gray at his temples appeared on the screen. "This is an emergency, Agent DM14," he began. "I've followed Bismarck halfway across the continent over the past few weeks, but I lost track of him at the port in Bergen. He disappeared right under my nose! I realized too late that he'd boarded the same ship you're on. I found out this morning, but I'm stuck on land!" There was a short pause as he adjusted the webcam lens, frowning. Then he went on. "You're very young, DM14. I need to know before I trust you with this delicate assignment: Are you capable of tailing a dangerous spy and noting down every suspicious move he makes?"

Dash stared nervously at the floor. "I don't know much about this sort of thing." He sighed.

"My detective career is going to go right down the tubes this time."

Agatha and Chandler were too busy watching the screen to respond. Watson had taken the opportunity to climb out of his cat carrier and hide in the closet. Agent AP36 assured them that the following morning, he'd arrive in Trondheim by train to take over the case. Then he described the spy's profile, which matched Agatha's prediction: He was a sixty-two-year-old German. "Bismarck" had used dozens of false identities, was constantly on the move, and always met his clients in public places with good surveillance like airports and train stations.

"He's careful and meticulous," the detective concluded. "You need to draw him out and follow his every move, Agent. Everything depends on you. I'll expect a full report when I meet you tomorrow at dawn. Over and out."

As the video clip finished, Dash looked at

Agatha. "Have you found the missing piece of the puzzle?" he asked hopefully.

She sat down, calmly lacing her fingers together. "Certainly," she said with a smile. "AP36 doesn't mention what Bismarck is spying on. The same information is missing from all the print files."

"It must be top secret," the butler judged. "All Master Dash has to do is keep a close eye on him for a few hours and report any suspicious activities. There's no need for him to know exactly what sort of espionage Bismarck is involved in."

"If you ask me," Agatha said, "there's only one important question: Why is Bismarck on board this particular ship? What do you think, colleagues?"

This sparked a lively discussion. According to Chandler, he must have found out he was being hunted by Eye International, and was trying to cut and run. Dash was convinced that the

only way to find out for sure was to interrogate Bismarck directly. But Agent AP36 had been clear that Dash should keep watch from a distance.

"Bismarck has an appointment with someone on the ship!" Agatha interrupted.

Seeing their confusion, she said, "There's a pattern to his behavior. Agent AP36 specified that Bismarck prefers to do business in crowded places for security reasons. Furthermore, you might remember that this cruise required us to register twenty days before departure. Our spy planned this trip well in advance. That means he has some kind of deal in the works."

At that moment, a bell rang. A smooth female voice with a Norwegian lilt announced over the intercom, "All passengers are kindly advised that the welcome dinner for new guests will start in thirty minutes."

"Dinner?" Dash sounded startled. "Is it that late already?"

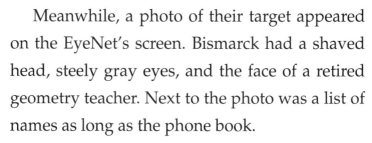

Meanwhile, a photo of their target appeared on the EyeNet's screen. Bismarck had a shaved head, steely gray eyes, and the face of a retired geometry teacher. Next to the photo was a list of names as long as the phone book.

"Erich Schmidt," read Dash, "aka Werner Kurtzmann, aka Hans Kleinhuber, aka Hermann Bauer . . . Wow, this guy must have a whole suitcase full of fake passports!"

"Why don't you run a search on your EyeNet?" said Agatha, giving her cousin a pat on the shoulder. "Try cross-referencing his list of fake identities with the passenger manifest."

Following her instructions, Dash opened the *King Arthur*'s database and brought up a list of the five thousand people on board.

"Unless Bismarck has created a brand-new identity," explained Agatha, "we'll be able to find out what deck he's staying on."

With a few taps of the keyboard, Dash checked the list of aliases against the passenger list. The results indicated that one Hermann Bauer was staying on Deck Eleven, in cabin 1188.

"Excellent!" Agatha exclaimed. "We can start on this case right away!"

Dash frowned, looking puzzled.

"The guests on Decks Ten and Eleven all eat in the same dining room, the Round Table," explained Agatha. "So we'll be able to see the

elusive Bismarck in person!"

"I'll need my tool kit!" Dash opened the closet.

Disturbed by the sudden intrusion, Watson flattened his ears and growled. Dash, who had no affection for cats, reached carefully into his suitcase and pulled out a plastic bag.

"Never get between a detective and his tools!" he told Watson.

Dash scattered the contents of the bag onto the bed: a chrome-plated lighter, some buttons, a pair of earrings, and a brooch. None of it looked too impressive.

"This isn't just any lighter," he said with a sly smile. "It contains a miniature video camera, perfect for filming without being caught."

Agatha picked up the coral earrings and studied them. "Hidden earbuds?" she asked.

"Exactly!" Dash grinned. "You'll wear them so that we can stay in touch. The buttons and brooch are ultralight microphones that can

transmit up to a thousand feet."

"Very impressive," admitted Chandler, hooking a button onto his collar.

"These are the tip of the iceberg," Dash said dreamily. "If you could see some of the gadgets at Eye International . . ."

The bell rang again and the same voice announced through the intercom, "All passengers are kindly advised that the welcome dinner will start in fifteen minutes. Please dress in evening attire."

"We're going to be late!" shrieked Dash, flinging himself at the closet as Watson hissed. "And where did I put my evening attire?"

Agatha and Chandler exchanged knowing looks, and left to get changed in their own cabins.

At seven o'clock on the dot, Agatha and the butler presented themselves at the Round Table dining room.

The ex-boxer wore an elegant dinner jacket.

Agatha had chosen a pearl-colored dress that complemented the coral earbuds and microphone-brooch.

"How luxurious," said Chandler, surveying the scene.

The enormous reception room housed a hundred perfectly set tables. The dazzling white of the china and tablecloths shone against the turquoise carpet. Large windows let in a flood of arctic sunlight.

"Over here!" called a distant voice. At table sixty-four, Edgar Mistery, Dash's father, waved vigorously. Kristi sat beside him, greeting them with a warm smile.

Edgar's new wife was a beautiful woman with short blond hair. Her eyes were as blue as the carpet, and she'd traded her usual sportswear for an elegant evening gown.

"Where's little Ilse?" asked Agatha, making herself comfortable.

"We've left her in the *King Arthur*'s daycare," trilled Kristi. "We thought she could do with a nap after all that activity."

"Speaking of which," said Edgar, "where's my son?"

"Oh, you know Dash, Uncle." Agatha smiled. "He's always late!"

Edgar chuckled, but Agatha was distracted by a bald man in his sixties taking his place, alone, at table fifty-eight, directly behind her uncle.

Agatha looked at Chandler, who'd also noticed Hermann Bauer's arrival.

"Here I am!" Dash cried breathlessly, rushing

to join them. He had combed his mop of dark hair and was wearing a black suit that actually fit. He sat down triumphantly next to his father.

Agatha excused herself for a moment, telling the others she wanted to look at the view out the windows. As soon as she got out of earshot, she tilted her head down and whispered into the brooch, "Dash, can you hear me? Just testing the microphone." Then she added, "Bismarck is sitting behind you. Also, you should know that your left collar button's undone." She turned to look back at Dash.

Dash's eyes widened and he adjusted his collar with a nervous gesture. Agatha smiled. Her cousin's gadgets were working perfectly.

A waiter placed a silver tray in the center of the table, mounded high with Norwegian smoked salmon and shellfish on ice. Edgar grabbed a fresh oyster and elbowed Dash. "What do you say, son? Let's have a contest to see who can eat the most!"

Dinner with a Spy

The dinner was cheerful. Agatha laughed at her uncle's jokes and chatted with Kristi, who was friendly and warm. Every so often, the aspiring mystery writer glanced over at Bauer's table. The bald spy seemed calm, but he had not eaten much. He wore a navy bow tie with his gray suit, and Agatha noted that he had a black leather briefcase beside him.

At around 8:45, the waiters served a succulent roast. As they ate, Uncle Edgar told them all how he'd met his third wife. "I saw her skate past and I slipped on the ice . . . I nearly broke my leg, but I'd do it again a thousand times. Thanks to that accident, I met my beloved Kristi!"

Chandler cleared his throat to catch Agatha's attention. She shot a look at table fifty-eight. Bismarck had picked up his briefcase and was heading toward the exit.

Blackjack Competition

*T*he spy crossed the room, stepping stealthily past a cart loaded with cream cakes and pastries. Then he slipped out the door and disappeared. Dash cast a worried glance at Agatha, who looked at her watch and exclaimed, "Oh, look how late it is!"

Dash nodded. Uncle Edgar and Kristi stared in amazement. What could make Dash Mistery leave before dessert?

"Dash, you wanted to go to the movies, remember? They're showing *Alien Hunt* in 4-D in the Percival Room." Agatha stood, grabbing her cousin's hand.

"L-later," he sputtered. "Save me an éclair!" They set off in hot pursuit of Hermann Bauer, with Chandler close behind.

Deck Nine was designed to look like a swanky European shopping street. Tourists crowded in throngs around its shops, cafés, and bars. It wasn't hard for the trio to shadow the German spy without being noticed—at least, that is, until he walked through a door under a dazzling neon sign that read Excalibur Casino.

"Just my luck!" moaned Dash. "He's gone into the one place on this whole ship where we can't follow him. Minors are prohibited from gambling! We won't be allowed to set foot in there!"

"Perhaps I can be of assistance, Master Dash," Chandler suggested.

They agreed that Chandler would continue to tail the spy inside the casino. Thanks to the microphone and earpieces, Agatha and Dash

would still be able to keep tabs on Bismarck. And the micro camera inside the lighter would film him as well, so Dash could watch the footage on his EyeNet.

The ex-boxer strolled inside with the swagger of a professional gambler. The children sat down at a table in the Sir Lancelot Café, opposite the casino. Agatha ordered a cup of tea and turned on her earbuds.

"Can you hear me, Miss?" said Chandler's voice through his hidden microphone.

"Loud and clear," Agatha replied. "Have you located Bauer?"

"He's sitting at a blackjack table. I'm looking for a good spot to position the camera. You should have a visual soon."

They could hear voices and rustling sounds in the background as he moved through the crowded casino. Then a loud ring of metal on metal exploded in the children's ears.

"What's that noise?" gasped Dash.

"Cascading money," Agatha said with confidence. "Slot machine! Am I right, Chandler?"

"You've got it," replied the butler. "I've traded some money for chips. I'll stand here and pretend to be playing the slots. Master Dash, can you connect to the camera feed?"

"Give me two seconds," Dash said, fiddling with the EyeNet. An image flashed on the screen: a high-angle view of the casino, richly carpeted in maroon.

"I've put the camera on top of the slot machine," Chandler explained.

On the screen, they could see Hermann Bauer sitting at a green upholstered table. There were three other players, and they were playing a fierce game of blackjack.

Chandler had chosen an excellent position. But he was too far from the table to catch

any conversation among the players amid all the crowd noise.

Dash squinted and carefully studied the scene. The spy and the other three players kept nodding at the croupier, who stood with his back to the camera.

"Do you have any idea how this game works?" he asked, scratching his head.

"It's pretty simple," Agatha said without moving her eyes from the screen. "Each player takes a turn to ask the croupier for a card, then adds up the points. The closest to twenty-one points without going over wins the jackpot."

There was a mountain of blue and red chips on the table. These players were betting heavily.

Bauer was the calmest of all, and so far he had only placed a small bet. The other three continued to raise their bets, adding more and more chips to their piles.

Agatha stared at each player, memorizing

their faces. There was an aristocratic man in his thirties to Bismarck's left. He had a pencil-thin beard and his blond hair was slicked back. He wore a white three-piece suit, with a smug smile pasted onto his face.

A powerfully built Asian man sat to the German's right. From the stiff bow he gave the croupier each time he accepted a bet, Agatha deduced he must be Japanese. He was dressed in black and wore a crocodile-leather jacket. His face was hard, and he had a visible scar across his left cheek.

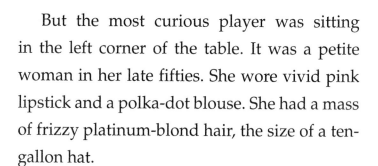

But the most curious player was sitting in the left corner of the table. It was a petite woman in her late fifties. She wore vivid pink lipstick and a polka-dot blouse. She had a mass of frizzy platinum-blond hair, the size of a ten-gallon hat.

Suddenly, there was another loud clatter of coins from the slot machine.

"Sorry about the racket," Chandler said. "It seems I've won a thousand pounds."

For the fourth time, the croupier cleared the table of the money the players had lost. None of them looked upset. With the exception of Bismarck, who continued to bet small change and quickly withdraw, the others continued to pile up more and more chips, making staggering bets.

"I don't know much about gambling," said Dash, confused. "But these players seem like real idiots. They're losing like crazy!"

"Perhaps the croupier is very skilled," Chandler replied.

Agatha sipped her tea. "Look closely, Dash. Bismarck is sitting on the sidelines watching the others, and they're betting huge sums of money without paying much attention to their cards at all."

"Are they just a bunch of weirdos who like to lose money?" Dash wondered aloud.

"No . . . They're just pretending to play!" explained Agatha. "The game of blackjack isn't important to any of them. The four of them are *communicating* with one another." Biting her lip with concentration, she added, "Why don't you launch the facial-recognition program on your EyeNet?"

"Done," said Dash. The computer promptly analyzed the players' faces, cross-referencing them with the long list of criminals, suspects, and mug shots contained on its hard drive.

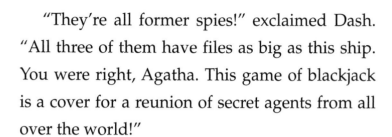

"They're all former spies!" exclaimed Dash. "All three of them have files as big as this ship. You were right, Agatha. This game of blackjack is a cover for a reunion of secret agents from all over the world!"

Agatha eyed the three files on the screen. The blond man dressed in white was English, and his name was Herbert Thackeray Miller. The Japanese gentleman went by the name Kentaro Takagi. The wacky woman with the polka-dot blouse was a Texan named Lilian Turner. The girl memorized all three names, then turned her attention back to the fake game of blackjack.

Just then, Lilian Turner flashed a triumphant smile. Annoyed, Miller thumped his fist on the green table. Even the impassive Asian man showed a brief flicker of disappointment.

"What just happened?" Dash stammered.

"It looks like the 'game' is over," replied Agatha. "And that, whatever was really going

on, Ms. Turner is the winner!"

The four players rose from their seats. It seemed the croupier was done for the moment as well. He nodded at the players and strolled off, adjusting his vest. The rest quickly moved away from the table, each going in different directions.

"Bismarck is heading for the exit," whispered Chandler.

"Great," said Dash, clearing the EyeNet screen. "We'll be able to track him in person!"

Just then he heard an unmistakable voice. "What are you doing here?" Edgar Mistery strode up to their café table.

"We were too late," Agatha improvised. "The movie had already started, and there were no seats left."

From the corner of her eye, she saw Bauer walk briskly out of Excalibur Casino and disappear into the crowd.

"So much the better." Edgar beamed. "You can

sit in a dark theater and watch movies at home! You're young, you need to move your bodies! How about we all go to Deck Ten? There's a big dance competition about to begin. Kristi went to change her shoes and check on Ilse. Let's meet her there."

Chandler appeared in the casino doorway. He was carrying a huge bag of chips and looking around in concern.

"Bauer went left," Agatha whispered into her brooch. The butler took off in the same direction to search for the spy. Dash was dying to join him, but Edgar was like a dog with a bone. He kept asking, "What do you say, kids? An intergenerational challenge: me and Kristi versus you two. A race to the last waltz!"

"Sorry, Dad," Dash muttered, becoming more and more agitated. "I can feel a big headache coming on . . ."

"No excuses, lazybones," said Edgar. "I won't settle for less! Anyway," he added with a teasing smile, "your adoring fans will be there. Have you forgotten those girls?"

"Don't worry, Master Dash," Chandler's voice spoke into his earpiece. "I overheard everything. I've just spotted Bismarck. He's in the middle of a crowd right in front of me. I suspect he's heading back to Deck Eleven. I can keep an eye on him for now. You'd better go with Mr. Edgar, or it will look suspicious. I'll keep you updated. Over and out."

Led by the exuberant Edgar Mistery, Dash and Agatha dragged their feet all the way to the ball.

Long-Distance Investigation

*O*n the Queen Guinevere Ballroom, thirty couples danced to the gentle rhythm of a waltz.

The orchestra performed each piece with expert precision, and the atmosphere was elegant. At Edgar's urging, Dash and Agatha tried a few turns under the envious eyes of the girls Dash had met at the pool that afternoon. Agatha didn't look happy.

"You may be a brilliant detective," Dash said with a smirk. "But you've got a lot to learn about dancing!"

"Who cares about dancing?" huffed Agatha. "We should focus on that group of spies."

"Chandler's got it covered for now. Try to relax and get into the groove!"

The orchestra launched into the opening bars of the "Blue Danube," a famous Viennese waltz by Johann Strauss.

Edgar Mistery approached the two children, bowing theatrically to Agatha. "Since my wife and dancing partner has not yet arrived, would you allow me the honor of this dance?"

Without waiting for a response, he led her into the middle of the floor, twirling her over the polished parquet. "And *that's* how it's done!" he bragged to Dash.

The music got faster and faster, becoming so loud that Agatha barely could hear Chandler's voice in her earbuds.

"Miss Agatha, Master Dash, sorry to disturb you . . . but we have a problem."

"Uh-oh," said Dash. "Have you lost track of Bismarck again?"

"He's in cabin 1188," replied Chandler. "But there is an issue. I regret to inform you that he is *deceased*."

"WHAT?" Dash shrieked so loudly that Agatha jumped. She continued to waltz with her uncle so as not to attract attention, but stole a glance over his shoulder at Dash. He stood frozen and pale at the edge of the dance floor, staring at her with wide eyes.

"That's impossible," he moaned into the microphone. "I'm supposed to be keeping an eye on him . . . and now this happens while I'm out dancing! I've really done it this time!"

"It's all my fault," Chandler said sadly. "If I hadn't let Bismarck get so far ahead of me, I would have caught his assassin red-handed!"

"Don't panic," Agatha whispered. "We'll find out what happened."

"All good, niece?" asked Edgar Mistery, raising an eyebrow at her twisted posture. "Why

are you looking down at the floor?"

"Just counting my steps," she replied, wriggling out of his grasp. Then she pointed to Dash, who was waving his arms in agitation. "But Dash looks upset. I think he might need dancing lessons as well."

"Great idea!" exclaimed her uncle, dancing with confident steps toward his son.

Dash shook his head, but the irrepressible Edgar dragged him onto the dance floor. "You'll see, son," he cried. "After one dance with me, you'll be an expert!"

While father and son were caught up in the waltz, Agatha moved away from the orchestra to continue the conversation with Chandler. Finding a quiet corner, she spoke into her brooch. "Can you hear me?"

"Loud and clear, Miss Agatha."

"Good. Tell me exactly what happened from the moment you lost sight of him."

Chandler spoke low in her ear. "I followed Bismarck to Deck Eleven, letting him get ahead so that he wouldn't spot me. Unfortunately, I lost track of him for a few minutes. Then I decided to check out his cabin, in hopes he'd gone back there. As I approached, I noticed the door was ajar . . . I pushed it open and saw his body sprawled on the bed. Unfortunately, there was nothing I could do: Hermann Bauer, aka Bismarck, was already dead."

Agatha raised her eyes to the dance floor, where Dash and his father were dancing to the "Blue Danube." Dash was shaking and stumbling all over the place, and Edgar corrected him eagerly.

"So you were the first to find Bismarck?" asked Agatha into the microphone.

"Exactly," said Chandler. "Nobody has noticed anything amiss, for now. The hall outside cabin 1188 is deserted. I'm the only one at the crime scene."

"That's for the best," said Agatha.

"Shall I use this opportunity to look for clues before the body is discovered and the crew raise the alarm?" asked the butler.

"Cou-could you film the scene with my micro camera?" stammered Dash's voice.

After an embarrassed pause, Chandler replied in dismay, "I'm afraid that's impossible, Master Dash. I must confess that in my hurry to follow Bismarck out of the casino, I left the lighter with the camera inside on top of the slot machine! This really isn't my night."

"Don't worry," Agatha reassured him. "Tell us what you can see at the moment. Begin with the corpse. Are you sure it was murder?"

"The victim is lying facedown," Chandler explained. "There are purple bruises around his neck . . ."

"So he was strangled," Agatha observed, tapping her nose.

It was a strange situation; they'd never had to analyze a crime scene . . . from a distance.

"Someone must have attacked him from behind," she continued. "Is there a murder weapon at the scene?"

"Unfortunately not." Chandler sighed. "There's no rope, or anything else that looks possible. The assassin must have been quick. There's no sign of a struggle."

"What else can you see around you?" asked the girl.

"There's an open briefcase on Bismarck's desk."

"Can you check what's inside and tell me if it's been broken into?" asked Agatha. "Be careful not to leave any sign that you've been there, especially fingerprints. We don't want to contaminate the crime scene."

"I've already put on latex gloves," he replied. "In case I need to touch anything in the room.

Regarding the briefcase, it seems to have been opened by force. There are signs of forced entry on the lock, though the scratches are very precise. It was likely done by a professional."

"The assassin sneaks into Bismarck's room," Agatha summarized. "Surprises him from behind and strangles him. He leaves the body on the bed, opens the briefcase, and steals its contents. Is there anything left in the briefcase?"

"Only the lining," the butler replied. "There is a small incision in it, right in the middle. The contents were stolen, just as you deduced, Miss. Whatever it was, it must have been very small."

"Like a flash drive containing some sort of secret information!" exclaimed Agatha, leaning against the ballroom wall.

The orchestra had finished the "Blue Danube" and started a waltz by Tchaikovsky, cheerful and upbeat. Dash and his father continued to whirl on the parquet floor.

"Anything else on the desk?" asked Agatha.

"An open envelope, already stamped. There's a name printed in capital letters on the front: Lilian."

Dash stepped on his father's foot in surprise, nearly sprawling across the floor. His father, unable to hear what was going on, laughed at his son's clumsiness and helped the boy steady himself.

"Lilian?" Dash's voice croaked in the earpieces. "Isn't that the name of the Texan ex-spy who was playing with Bismarck at the casino?"

Agatha cast her mind back to the frizzy-haired woman with the polka-dot blouse. She recalled her look of triumph just before they all got up from the table.

"Lilian Turner," she said. "She won that bizarre game of blackjack! Bauer was probably writing her a message when he was attacked. Chandler, is it possible to check inside the envelope

without leaving any traces?"

"Certainly," replied the ex-boxer. They heard a faint rustling in the background, then the butler spoke. "There's a sheet of writing paper inside, but it's completely blank!"

"The victim evidently wanted to contact Ms. Turner," the girl reflected, adjusting the microphone brooch on her dress. "But why would he send her a blank sheet of paper?"

"If I had to guess," Chandler said, "I'd say it's some sort of signal. Or perhaps the letter contains a message written in invisible ink. Too bad we can't remove it from the scene of the crime. If we were able to run some tests on it, we might find something interesting."

"Leave it where it is," said Agatha. "Tell me, what else do you see?"

Chandler rapidly examined the cabin. The closet and drawers had been ransacked, and the small window was open.

"The culprit must have escaped through it," the butler said. "He obviously didn't want to run the risk of encountering any other passengers as he was leaving the scene of the crime."

"What's outside the window?" asked Agatha.

"A terrace with lifeboats," said Chandler. "From there, it would be possible to get back inside the *King Arthur* through one of the service doors . . . and disappear without a trace!"

"Speaking of traces," Agatha said, "it's probably best if you get away from there, too. The assassin might return to check on the scene. Or worse, someone might surprise you in the victim's cabin and think you're a suspect!"

"Right away," agreed Chandler. "I'll pull the cabin's alarm on my way out so the crew are notified."

Agatha raised her eyes to the dance floor. Kristi had finally arrived.

Uncle Edgar saw her at once, and swooped over to greet her. Freed from his father's attention, Dash rushed to his cousin. He was breathless with shock.

"What a mess!" he panted, leaning against the wall. "Now what do we do?"

"Rejoin Chandler," Agatha promptly replied.

"The alarm is activated," the butler's voice confirmed in their earpieces. "I'm going down to Deck Seven, above the great hall. I'll wait for you there."

"Perfect!" Dash turned toward the exit.

"Had enough, little man?" Edgar called from behind. Dash rolled his eyes in exasperation. Then he turned around, flashing his brightest smile.

"You win, Dad," he said. "You're unbeatable on the dance floor!"

"Plus we're a bit tired," said Agatha, pretending to stifle a yawn. "I think we could do with some sleep."

"Young people today!" gloated Edgar Mistery. "Your old man's got twice as much energy! You need more exercise, boy. It takes next to nothing to wipe you out!"

"Oh, this is by Chopin!" cried Kristi, as the orchestra started to play a new waltz. "Leave the poor kids alone and let's dance, darling!"

Edgar gave his wife a gallant kiss on the hand. Then the two lovebirds swept away, leaving the children free to meet Chandler.

Ms. Turner's Confession

*A*gatha cast an eye over the railing of Deck Seven. The *King Arthur*'s vast hall spread out below them. Even though it was already after eleven, the ship was still crowded with tourists going in and out of shops. They had no idea that there'd been a murder on board the ship.

"No signal," Dash grumbled, raising his eyes from the EyeNet. "The communications satellite seems to have gone haywire. I can't get a connection to London."

He'd spent several minutes trying to contact Eye International headquarters to report what had happened. Agent AP36 was out of reach on a moving train, so they'd have to fend for themselves.

"It's strange that the news of the crime hasn't spread yet," commented Chandler.

"Usually in cases like this, the captain contacts the authorities in the nearest port," said Agatha, who'd read several mysteries set on ocean liners. "Bismarck's body will be taken from the ship in Trondheim tomorrow morning as discreetly as possible, to avoid ruining the cruise for other passengers."

"What am I going to tell Agent AP36?" asked Dash.

"The name of the murderer, if we act quickly enough," Agatha replied. "The culprit must be one of the three former spies who met Bismarck at the casino."

"Yeah, but what were the four of them scheming?" groaned Dash.

"There's one way to find out: Ask them!" said

Agatha. "We'll interrogate all three and find out who killed Bismarck."

"Who do you suggest we track down first?" Chandler asked.

"Let's start with Lilian Turner," Agatha replied. "Her name was written on the letter the victim left. Dash, what does her file say?"

Dash opened the file and began to read.

"Fifty-nine years old, born in Dallas, Texas. Ex–CIA agent, highly decorated. She left the American secret services eight years ago for health reasons. She has chronic rheumatism that forced her to take an early retirement."

Agatha and Chandler exchanged puzzled glances. Their brightly dressed suspect seemed far from retired.

Dash went on. "But she hasn't been idle. It seems that, like Bismarck, she put her experience to use as a private spy for rich corporations."

Checking the roster of passengers, Dash

discovered that Ms. Turner was staying on Deck Five, cabin 577. The three headed briskly in that direction.

"I don't think she's in her cabin," announced Chandler after knocking a couple of times.

"There's no way we'll be able to find her," Dash groaned. "This ship is as big as a city."

"I bet she's on Deck Six," said Agatha, flashing a confident smile.

Dash and Chandler stared at her, wide-eyed. She took off down the hall and the other two followed.

"At this time of night," Agatha explained, "most of the attractions are closed. But just down these stairs on Deck Six, there's one that stays open till midnight: the spa! Lilian Turner suffers from chronic rheumatism, right? The warm air of a steam room is just the thing for those kinds of complaints."

Moments later, the group reached the glass

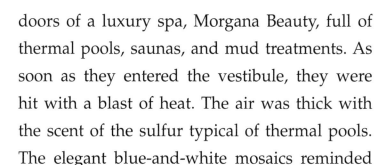

doors of a luxury spa, Morgana Beauty, full of thermal pools, saunas, and mud treatments. As soon as they entered the vestibule, they were hit with a blast of heat. The air was thick with the scent of the sulfur typical of thermal pools. The elegant blue-and-white mosaics reminded Agatha of Roman baths.

"We've forgotten one detail," said Dash. "We don't have our swimsuits. We can't go inside unless we're wearing them!"

"We'll just have to pretend, then," said Agatha with a grin. She slipped off her shoes and reached for a peg rack where a dozen white terry cloth robes hung. She pulled one on and secured the belt, perfectly hiding her dress. Chandler kicked off his shoes and rolled his pants up to the knees.

"We'll liquefy in this heat!" complained Dash, cloaking himself in a terry cloth robe.

As soon as the butler was ready, the trio headed toward the pool.

Inside, it was ninety degrees, and the humidity was as high as in an Amazonian rain forest. Dash flushed as red as a pepper, dripping with sweat. Chandler, however, somehow maintained his immaculate air.

"Excellent deduction, Miss," he commented, nodding discreetly toward a corner of the pool. "There's our first suspect."

There were still a dozen guests in the spa. Apart from the rest, on the edge of the pool, sat Lilian Turner. She was wearing a polka-dot swimsuit, and her pouf of hair was covered with a hot-pink swim cap.

The trio walked toward her carefully. Dash passed a hand across his forehead to wipe away beads of sweat. He was trying to think up a way to approach her.

But it was the Texan who made the first move. She raised her blue eyes to Chandler and flashed him a grin. "Howdy there, colleague. How's

your secret mission going?"

"Excuse me?" muttered the butler, taken aback.

"Come on," laughed Lilian. "I worked for the CIA for thirty years. Even if I'm *almost* retired, I know a fellow spy when I see one."

Agatha smiled. This woman's powers of observation were remarkable.

"Even a child would have realized you were playing the slots just to keep an eye on our little ole game," she continued. "Am I mistaken, or did you leave your micro camera behind? And you Brits always brag about your precision." Lilian Turner stood up with difficulty, turning to face them. "So what do you want with me, pardner?"

"We're not spies," said Dash resolutely. "I'm a detective from Eye International. We're here to deliver you to the ship's captain: I'm certain that you're the one who murdered Hermann Bauer!"

Ms. Turner raised an eyebrow in confusion. Agatha explained the situation.

When the woman heard about Bismarck's death, her face fell. "Poor man." She sighed. "He seemed nice."

"Calling him *nice* won't get you off the hook," said Dash drily.

"Why in tarnation would I want to kill him? I won the auction for Bismarck's goods. I don't have any motive to kill him."

"W-wait up," stammered Dash. "What auction? What goods?"

"Don't tell me you didn't know!" Lilian looked startled. "Bismarck brought us all on the cruise to sell some valuable information . . . to the highest bidder!"

"That solves the blackjack mystery!" exclaimed Agatha. "Your bets weren't related to the game at all . . . You were raising bids to buy Bismarck's information!"

"What information?" said Dash. "What did he want to sell?"

"An engine prototype," replied Lilian, starting to grin. "Or the formula for a new super-tanning sunscreen. Or maybe the schematics for a next-generation cell phone. In any case, it's nothing criminal. We all specialize in trading top secret industrial information. But we're just the middlemen . . . None of us knew what Bismarck was selling. That's our rich employers' business!"

"Yeah, so, who's your rich employer?" Dash interrupted.

"That's a professional secret, buddy!" Ms. Turner laughed. "If you think I'll tell you, you're dreaming!" Then her face became serious. "We didn't do anything illegal. The auction was conducted in the usual way, even if it was top secret. I made the best offer, and Bismarck's information was mine. We made an appointment. Before he left the ship, he was going to give me a flash drive with the information, and I would have paid the amount we'd agreed on. But somebody did him in and stole it first. What a mess . . . The boss isn't going to be pleased when he hears this news!"

"As far as I'm concerned, you could still be the assassin." Dash sounded suspicious. "Let's say you decided not to pay Bismarck at the last minute . . . but you got your precious information all the same. That'd be worth . . ."

"Lilian Turner is innocent!" declared Agatha firmly.

Dash stared at her, stunned.

"I already knew it couldn't be her. When we were watching the video, I could see she was petite. She would barely have reached Bismarck's shoulders. Not only that, but she suffers from rheumatism. How could she have surprised the victim from behind and strangled him?"

"Well . . . ," Dash admitted, scratching his head. "You have some good points."

"Brains of the outfit, huh?" Lilian Turner looked at Agatha, impressed. "I'll tell you exactly what happened. One of the other two bidders in the auction couldn't face losing, so he decided to murder Bismarck and steal the flash drive that I rightfully won. They're the two suspects you ought to investigate!"

Lilian leaned closer, speaking in a conspiratorial whisper. "Miller, the young Brit,

Ms. Turner's Confession

is kind of a hothead . . . but he seems harmless to me. The more likely suspect is that Japanese fellow. He's a shadowy sort. He's a martial-arts fanatic and spends all his time working out at the gym. Believe me, he doesn't take defeat well. I could be wrong, of course . . . But I'd bet my hat he's the one who attacked Bismarck and stole *my* flash drive!"

"There's only one way to find out if you're right, Ms. Turner," said Dash. "Let's go find him!"

"I'll join you!" said the peppery Texan. "I bought that top secret info, and I want it back."

"Thanks for the offer," said Agatha. "But it would be best if you went back to your cabin for now. If the culprit sees us together, he might suspect something's up. We need to be very discreet and solve this mystery by tomorrow morning!"

The three detectives and the ex-spy said their

good-byes in the spa's locker room.

Dash Mistery could not get his robe off fast enough. Beneath it, his whole suit was drenched in sweat.

Ninety-Nine Dragons

"Kentaro Takagi," said Dash, bringing up his profile on the EyeNet. "Forty-one years old, born in Okinawa. Ex–secret agent from Naicho, Tokyo's intelligence service. Expelled six years ago for reasons that were never revealed, he now works for a variety of private citizens. A black belt in nine martial arts, he practices Bushido, the ancient art of the samurai, which is a true life philosophy. He seems like a real tough guy!"

The three detectives went straight to the place they expected to find Kentaro: the Parsifal Dojo, the *King Arthur*'s biggest gym.

Inside, there were tennis and racquetball courts, and even a skating rink.

Agatha, Dash, and Chandler sneaked into the men's locker room. There was only one set of clothes hanging up, those of the last person visiting the gym. Agatha recognized the black outfit and the crocodile jacket that Kentaro Takagi had been wearing at the casino a few hours earlier.

"This guy isn't going to be easy to crack," said Dash with a nervous laugh.

"Well, we'll have to get him talking one way or another," Agatha replied. "Look what I found in his jacket pocket!"

She held up a small rectangular object, plated in gold. It was a flash-drive stick.

"It's exactly the same size as the slit in the lining of the briefcase," said Chandler. "It must be the flash drive that the culprit stole from Bismarck . . . after he murdered him!"

They entered the gym on tiptoe. It was deserted, and a profound silence hung in the air. There was only one guest, immobile in the middle of the room. He was sitting with legs crossed on a mat, wearing a red silk kimono. He had his back to the trio.

He appeared to be contemplating the view out the window. Even though it was late, the sky shone with luminous twilight. The arctic sun would soon rise again over the sea.

Dash shot a knowing look at Agatha and Chandler. Then he approached on tiptoe.

"Don't take another step!" commanded Takagi without turning around.

Dash froze.

"What do you want?" snarled the Japanese athlete.

Dash gathered his courage. "Takagi, we're taking you straight to the ship's captain. You murdered Hermann Bauer, admit it!"

The man did not move a muscle. Agatha and Chandler stepped forward. Takagi stood up in one swift movement, turning to face them. His face was fierce. A split second later, a wry smile crossed his face as he sized up Dash.

"You're . . . giving an order to *me*?" he sneered. "Listen, you impudent brat, how do you plan to do that? Get lost, or there'll be trouble!"

"Don't make us use force," said Chandler, taking a step forward.

Takagi did not lose his cool. Loosening his belt, he slipped off the kimono. His chest and arms were covered in multicolored Japanese tattoos, in which dragons, fish, and cherry blossoms

intertwined. His muscles rippled like serpents.

Unimpressed, Chandler took another step forward.

"You want to face me in combat?" Kentaro hissed. "Do not be pathetic!" He cracked his knuckles, took a deep breath, and flexed his muscles. "You stand no chance against me! My body is as flexible as bamboo and as strong as steel. My hand is more deadly than a *katana*, the lethal Japanese sword!"

"Less chat, if you don't mind," said Chandler, raising his fists.

The warrior gave a deep bow. His eyes blazed.

"Very well, sir. I respect your courage! I will allow you the honor of succumbing to my most powerful move: the Ninety-Nine Dragon Punch! A lethal technique, passed down through the centuries by an ancient secret order of warrior monks! Only a select few have ever had the privilege of . . ."

But Kentaro did not finish his sentence. Chandler, impatient, gave him a left hook to the face. The Japanese man staggered backward and fell to the ground, unconscious.

"I beg your pardon," said the butler. "But we're in a bit of a hurry."

Takagi recovered his senses a few minutes later. By then, Chandler had dragged him to the locker room and propped him on a bench while Dash procured a bag of ice to help with his black eye.

"Ah, why didn't you finish me off?" Takagi lamented. "Defeat is worse than death for those of us who follow Bushido, the samurai code of honor!"

"Enough of that," Dash cut him off.

"Now confess: You killed Bismarck and stole the secret files on the flash drive, didn't you?"

"Lies!" thundered Takagi. "I don't know what you're talking about. I accepted my defeat at the auction with honor. Then I went straight to the gym to meditate and purify my spirit. I've been here ever since."

"And yet we found this in your jacket," said Dash, holding up the gold flash drive. Takagi grimaced.

"I've never seen that before," he said coldly. "Someone must have put it there to frame me."

"Dash, try connecting the flash drive to the EyeNet and see what's on it," said Agatha thoughtfully. "Maybe Mr. Takagi is telling the truth."

Dash immediately followed her instructions. In seconds, the EyeNet scanned the contents. A look of amazement flashed over the young detective's face.

"I—I can't believe it," he stammered. "It's empty!"

"Maybe the culprit deleted the data after he copied it?" Chandler hypothesized.

"If so, the EyeNet would be able to recover it," replied Dash. "But this flash drive is brand-new. It's been analyzed by one of my programs. I guarantee you that it's never been used or tampered with!"

"That means there are two possibilities," Agatha concluded. "Either this isn't the stolen flash drive . . . or it *was* the one in Bismarck's case, but it was just a decoy! The top secret information he was selling could still be hidden somewhere else."

"Okay, but that doesn't explain what this was doing in Takagi's pocket!" Dash noted. "And he's definitely strong enough to have strangled Hermann Bauer."

"I'm being set up, I tell you!" exclaimed

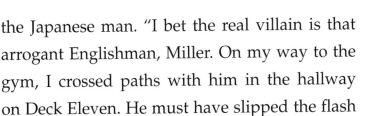

the Japanese man. "I bet the real villain is that arrogant Englishman, Miller. On my way to the gym, I crossed paths with him in the hallway on Deck Eleven. He must have slipped the flash drive into my pocket then. What a snake!"

Kentaro Takagi's eyes burned with contempt. "That coward must have attacked Bismarck. Then, when he realized the flash drive he'd stolen was blank, he decided to get rid of it, and transfer the blame to me at the same time. Miller is a former thief, very skilled with his hands. He's set me up!"

"Why should we believe you?" Dash pressed. "Is there anyone who can testify that you left the casino and came straight here . . . without paying a little visit to the victim's cabin first?"

"As I said before," Agatha interrupted, "I think Mr. Takagi is telling the truth. He couldn't have killed Bismarck!"

"Why not?" grumbled Dash.

"I read a book about the Bushido samurai code a while ago. Bismarck was strangled by someone who attacked him from behind, right? But for a Japanese warrior to attack an enemy from behind would be extremely dishonorable!"

"I'd rather die!" cried Takagi. "I am no coward who attacks with such treachery. I always meet enemies face to face!"

"So, if Takagi is innocent," Chandler considered, "then the assassin has to be . . ."

"Miller!" cried Dash. "Let's go find him!"

Takagi stood, giving a deep bow to the ex-boxer. "Noble warrior, you beat me in a fair fight and punished me for my arrogance. I wish to remedy my mistake! I will follow you faithfully and help you flush out this snake, Miller!"

Chandler scratched his head. He was much more at ease taking orders than giving them.

Agatha told Takagi that it would be best if Miller didn't see them together. "It gives us the

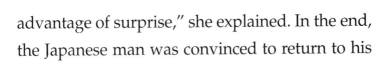

advantage of surprise," she explained. In the end, the Japanese man was convinced to return to his cabin.

The three detectives made their way to Deck Four, where they found the cabin of the last of their three suspects, Herbert Thackeray Miller. They arrived at his door and found it locked.

"Here we go again." Dash sighed. "Who knows where he's gone?"

"In this case," said Agatha, "the Englishman's absence gives us a certain advantage. If we are going by elimination, we can assume he must be the culprit. So if we can sneak into his room, we can search for proof to incriminate him beyond any doubt."

"Do you want me to break down the door?" asked Chandler.

"That won't be necessary," said Dash, eyeing the electronic lock. "Thanks to one of the apps on my EyeNet, I can get us inside in no time!"

The Murder Weapon

*T*he magnetic lock on Herbert Miller's cabin opened with a sharp *click.*

Dash held up the EyeNet, flashing a smug smile. "See? Opening doors on this ship is child's play!"

The room reflected the Englishman's vanity: the air was thick with eau de cologne. There were scented candles and floral bouquets on the nightstand. The cabin was perfectly tidy. Agatha noticed just one thing out of place: a black silk tie lying on the carpet.

She took a tissue, bent over, and picked it up, being careful not to leave fingerprints. "It

looks like Miller must have been wearing this for a while," she commented. "It's crumpled and twisted in a strange way."

The tie had two loops at the ends. The fabric looked stretched, as if it had been subjected to strong tension.

Meanwhile, Dash searched the room.

"Everything looks in order," he commented. "Are we sure he's really the murderer?"

"I'm sure of one thing," whispered Agatha, showing him the tie. "This was used to strangle Bismarck. In other words, dear colleagues, we have found the murder weapon!"

"Murder weapon?" said a shrill voice with a posh English accent. "Who are you, and what are you doing here?"

The two children and Chandler turned. Young Herbert Miller had just appeared in the cabin doorway. He was still wearing his spotless white suit. He stared at them, wide-eyed and anxious.

"Miller, we're taking you to the ship's captain!" cried Dash. "You're guilty of murdering Hermann Bauer!"

"M-murder?" he stammered. "What the deuce are you talking about?"

"Don't play dumb," said Dash. "After you lost the auction, you went to Bismarck's cabin, strangled him, and stole a flash drive containing top secret information. When you discovered that the flash drive was blank, you slipped it into Takagi's pocket. Then you got rid of the murder weapon, throwing it here on the rug . . . Am I right?"

"You're dead wrong!" snapped Miller. "It's true, after I lost the auction, I left the Excalibur Casino immediately. But a gentleman knows how to accept defeat . . . I took in a bracing breath of sea air, and went back to the casino straightaway to play blackjack with more skillful opponents."

"So why is the tie that was used to strangle

Bismarck here in your cabin?" asked Agatha.

"I have no idea!" Miller said, throwing his arms wide. "Someone must have put it here without my knowledge. It couldn't be mine. Check my wardrobe, if you don't believe me."

Chandler opened the closet door. Jackets, shirts, pants, and ties were neatly hung inside . . . all in shades of white, cream, and ivory.

"I can't abide black!" exclaimed Miller. "Loathe that color. I never wear it."

"The fact that the tie doesn't match doesn't prove a thing," said Dash, pointing a finger. "You could have taken the black one out of Bismarck's own wardrobe!"

"I don't think so," said Agatha. "I've only seen Bismarck wearing a bow tie."

"There were no neckties in his wardrobe," confirmed Chandler. "Only more bow ties!"

"Besides," said Agatha, "you just proved how easy it is to force locks on the *King Arthur*'s

cabins. The real assassin wouldn't have had any trouble opening the door and throwing the tie on the rug!"

"The girl's right!" Miller said. "I'm completely at your disposal. I would like to help you find whoever killed Bismarck. I can assure you that I had nothing to do with the matter!"

Discouraged, Dash sat down, holding his head in his hands. "It's official. I'm going to be kicked out of school! Three suspects and they all have alibis . . . I just don't get it!"

"There are two possibilities," said Agatha. "Either one of them lied and is really the culprit . . . or we've been on the wrong track all along, and the person who killed Bismarck *wasn't* one of the three blackjack players!"

"We just need to find out who owns that tie," observed Chandler.

"Or simply remember who wore a black tie during the auction," replied Agatha, chewing her

lip. Then her face lit up. "Of course! The camera!"

"What camera?" asked Herbert Miller, stunned.

"The one Chandler left on the slot machine in the Excalibur Casino," she replied. "It's still there and has probably been recording all night!"

"Yes!" Dash confirmed, patting his pocket. "That battery should last for days. Everything it has filmed is saved on the EyeNet."

Dash pulled out the titanium device and turned it on. The camera had recorded four and a half hours of footage.

"Go back to the blackjack game," Agatha suggested. Dash complied with a few taps on the touch screen. The scene reappeared before the detectives' eyes. Bismarck was wearing a bow tie, just as Agatha remembered. Ms. Turner, of course, was not wearing a tie. Herbert Miller was wearing the same ivory tie he still had on, and Kentaro Takagi had no tie at all.

"You see? None of them could be the culprit!" said Agatha.

"But then, who is?" Dash sounded worried.

Agatha kept her eyes on the screen as the recorded game ended. Ms. Turner got up, looking triumphant, while the other two walked away disappointed. Then Bismarck left. The last to leave was the croupier. He turned toward the camera for a brief instant.

Long enough for them to see that he was wearing a black silk tie.

"Skip forward ten minutes or so," said Agatha.

Dash obliged. After his break, the croupier resumed his place at the table and continued dealing to other tourists on board the *King Arthur*.

But his tie had disappeared.

"It makes perfect sense that he wouldn't be wearing it," Agatha said slowly. "Because it's right here in my hand . . . It was the croupier who strangled Bismarck!"

"But who is he?" asked Dash.

"And why Hermann Bauer?" asked Miller.

"Try running that facial-recognition program again," Agatha urged.

Dash went back to work on his EyeNet. In moments, a file on the mysterious croupier came up on the screen.

"Pablo Navarro, thirty-six years old. Spanish citizen, born in Barcelona. It says he's an ex–secret agent for the Spanish intelligence service, Centro Nacional de Inteligencia. Fired six years ago for

undisclosed reasons. Master of disguise, he's famous for subterfuge. He usually conducts his business in secret, without disclosing his presence to his competitors . . ."

"In our business," Herbert confirmed, "everyone knows about Pablo Navarro . . . but only by reputation! Few have ever seen his face. Bismarck must have contacted him about the auction as well. But Navarro participated in disguise, pretending to be the croupier. All without our knowledge!"

Agatha continued to study the footage on the EyeNet.

"The times match up. During his break, Navarro followed Bismarck back to his cabin and committed the crime. Then he searched the briefcase and stole the flash drive. Once he realized it was blank, he hid in it Kentaro's pocket, so he must have gone to the gym . . ."

She pointed to the cabin door. "Finally he

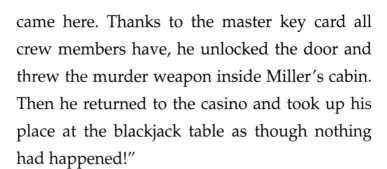

came here. Thanks to the master key card all crew members have, he unlocked the door and threw the murder weapon inside Miller's cabin. Then he returned to the casino and took up his place at the blackjack table as though nothing had happened!"

"What a creep!" hissed the English ex-spy. "He tried to frame me for murder!"

"You're wrong," said Agatha. "If he had wanted to incriminate you, or one of the other auction participants, he would have acted differently."

Dash frowned again.

Agatha gave him a smile and continued. "If Navarro had wanted to pin the blame on Miller, he would have left the flash drive here with the murder weapon, don't you think? In which case we would have no doubt about Miller's guilt."

"Well, yes," said Dash, nodding. "So why didn't he do that?"

The Murder Weapon

"He didn't care about framing a colleague. His objective wasn't to pin the blame on one of you three. He only wanted to muddy the waters. Mess up the investigation and perhaps cause you three to suspect one another!"

"But why?" asked Dash.

"To buy time!" exclaimed Agatha. "And that's not good news . . ."

She jumped up and strode to the cabin door. "Don't you get it? We're docking at Trondheim in just a few hours . . . Navarro is planning to leave the *King Arthur* as soon as he can and cover his tracks!"

Dash jumped to his feet. "We don't have much time to discover his hiding place!"

"I think we'll need everyone's help!" exclaimed Agatha, turning to Miller. "Contact Lilian Turner and Kentaro Takagi. Meet us at the casino. Maybe Navarro is still dealing blackjack!"

When the three detectives and three ex-spies

met on Deck Nine, the Excalibur's neon sign was turned off, but the shuttered door was propped open.

"The casino's about to close," Miller said with a grimace.

"There'll be nobody left but the cleaning crew," said Lilian Turner.

"So much the better!" Dash said happily. "Nobody will be around to make a fuss if we minors go and take a look."

Just then a familiar voice sounded behind him.

"Son, what are you doing up? I thought you went to bed hours ago!"

Edgar Mistery was standing behind them, with Kristi on his arm.

The Final Bluff

*E*dgar Mistery approached, grinning. Sensing Dash's discomfort, the three spies retreated, feigning an air of indifference.

"Well, well, well," Edgar said cheerfully. "Living the high life, aren't we? Planning to introduce us to these lovely people?"

"We have a problem, Uncle," Agatha said with a worried frown. "Watson escaped from my cabin. We've been looking for him for hours. These three kind people"—she pointed at Turner, Takagi, and Miller—"are helping us search!"

"We'll help you, too!" Edgar promptly exclaimed.

"We don't need your help, Dad." Dash cut him off, blocking the entrance to the casino. "We just saw him go in here. Too many people will only scare him away. We'll see you two and Ilse at breakfast tomorrow!"

The casino was deserted. The slot machines had been turned off, and the only people left inside were a couple of cleaners, vacuuming the maroon carpet. Chandler recovered the camera as Miller approached the two cleaners to ask about Pablo Navarro.

The young Englishman returned to the group, his head lowered. "Bad luck! Navarro was at the blackjack table until twenty minutes ago. Then he disappeared!"

"We should split up to look for him," said Ms. Turner. "I'll check to see if he's returned to his cabin!"

"I'll check all the bars that are still open," suggested Herbert. "Maybe he went to get

something to eat after his shift."

"I'll search the outside decks and the lifeboats. If I find him there, I'll take him out with my dragon punch!" Kentaro exclaimed with a bow.

"We'll check out the covered decks," concluded Agatha. "Stay in touch. The first to find the assassin will let the others know, agreed?"

"I'll talk to your earrings," said Ms. Turner, winking.

The group split up. The children and Chandler went up to Deck Ten. It was past two in the morning, and the ship was practically deserted. Only a few night owls were up roaming the halls.

"This ship is a maze!" exclaimed Dash. "And it's less than three hours until we dock in Trondheim. Navarro could be hiding anywhere by now, in the hold or some other area off-limits to the public . . . We'll never find him!"

"I'm afraid Master Dash may be right this time," Chandler observed. "It would take a

stroke of exceptional luck to come across the fugitive before the ship docks."

"Well, there's one consolation," Dash said bitterly. "The assassin may get away with murder . . . but he wasn't able to get his hands on Bismarck's top secret information."

"The information!" Agatha's eyes widened. "Of course! Why didn't I think of that earlier?"

Dash and Chandler turned to face her. Her face lit up, radiant.

"Bismarck's flash drive was just a front," she explained. "The information is still hidden somewhere else. Probably inside his cabin!"

"Perhaps." Chandler nodded. "But what does that have to do with our search?"

"Don't you understand?" she said. "Pablo Navarro would never leave the *King Arthur* without taking it with him. As in the best mystery tradition, the killer will return to the scene of the crime!"

She strode toward a flight of stairs leading up to Deck Eleven.

"Tell the others, Dash! We'll find our culprit in Bismarck's cabin right now!"

Five minutes later, the three detectives arrived outside cabin 1188. The hall was deserted and the cabin door slightly ajar. Two voices could be heard from within. Agatha approached on tiptoe, leaning forward to peer through the crack.

The room was exactly as Chandler had described it. Bismarck's briefcase sat on the desk. The German spy's body was still on the bed, but it had been wrapped in a plastic body bag. Standing in the center of the room were two men.

Agatha recognized both of them.

The first was the captain of the *King Arthur*, who'd been at the welcome party. He was a stocky man with a shaved head, dressed in his official uniform. He looked upset.

The second was Pablo Navarro. His hair

was slicked back and he had a thin mustache. He was still wearing his croupier outfit, and his eyes darted around the room, as though he were trying to find something hidden.

"That's all I know, *Señor* Captain," he said with a strong Spanish accent. "I only just met this poor fellow at the blackjack table a few hours ago . . ."

The captain snorted in annoyance. "You're wasting my time! First you tell me you have evidence relating to the murder of Mr. Bauer. Then you tell me that you won't share your

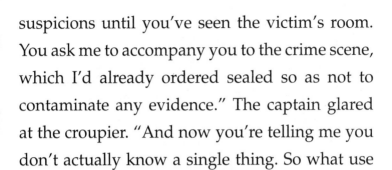

suspicions until you've seen the victim's room. You ask me to accompany you to the crime scene, which I'd already ordered sealed so as not to contaminate any evidence." The captain glared at the croupier. "And now you're telling me you don't actually know a single thing. So what use are you?"

"Simple," said Agatha, pushing the door open and entering. "Your croupier came here to find out where Bauer hid the information he tried to steal after murdering him! And he needed you to reopen the sealed crime scene."

The false croupier's jaw tensed almost imperceptibly.

"And who are you, Miss?" asked the captain.

"We're agents of Eye International," Dash declared as he entered, followed by Chandler. "And we can prove that this man killed Hermann Bauer!"

The captain raised his eyebrows in surprise.

Pablo Navarro ran a hand through his gelled hair and gave a nervous laugh. "Come on, Captain . . . You can't take these two *niños* seriously!"

"I've never been more serious," said Dash, his voice hard-edged. "Captain, this man is a murderer. He used his necktie to strangle Bauer . . . the one he's no longer wearing!" He held up the evidence.

"Estupidez!" growled Navarro. "Nonsense! I will not allow these two children to drag my good name through the mud!"

"There's no point pretending," said Agatha coldly. "We know everything, Navarro. We even managed to find out where the information you tried to steal is hidden."

She pointed at Bismarck's briefcase. "The files weren't on that flash drive . . . but inside the briefcase lining itself!"

At these words, the croupier reacted like

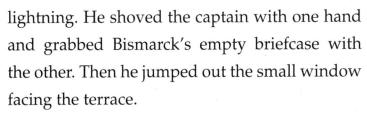

lightning. He shoved the captain with one hand and grabbed Bismarck's empty briefcase with the other. Then he jumped out the small window facing the terrace.

The captain lay sprawled on the ground, paralyzed with surprise. Dash and Chandler stepped over him and climbed through the open window. The last person to leave cabin 1188 was Agatha, who paused at the desk for a moment before she went out.

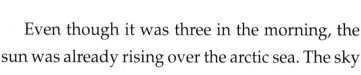

Even though it was three in the morning, the sun was already rising over the arctic sea. The sky shone red, pink, and gray. Impressive green swirls of light shimmered above the horizon. It was the famous aurora borealis, the northern lights.

Pablo Navarro was running toward a service entrance to the ship. Just before he went through it, he turned to face his pursuers.

"Thanks for the tip, *niños!*" he shouted triumphantly, waving the briefcase. "Now I've got my hands on Bismarck's information, and all I have to do is escape. We'll be docking before you can blink! *Adios!*"

The door opened behind him, and Herbert Miller, Kentaro Takagi, and Lilian Turner spilled onto the terrace.

"Hands up and surrender, Navarro!" the Englishman yelled.

"Or prepare for a fight!" thundered the Japanese man.

"Either way, you're Texas toast!" Lilian Turner laughed.

Agatha, Dash, and Chandler approached Navarro. The fake croupier was surrounded. He fell to his knees, whipped open the briefcase, and tore at the foam lining in search of Bismarck's secret files.

"You're wasting your time," Agatha said with a smile. "The microchip containing the information isn't in the briefcase lining. I lied to make you give yourself away. Call it a bluff, *señor*."

Chandler and Takagi swooped down on the fugitive, restraining both arms.

The captain came out to join them, accompanied by two security guards.

"Now, can someone please tell me what's happening on my ship?" he cried.

While Chandler and Dash filled him in, Agatha and the three former spies stepped away.

"The murderer's been caught," Miller said with a frown. "But there's still one mystery left. What became of the top secret information?"

Agatha smiled, pulled an envelope out of her jacket, and gave it to Lilian Turner. It was the same one Chandler had found at the crime scene.

"I collected it from the desk in his cabin," she explained. "Your name is written on top. I think poor Bismarck addressed it to you."

Ms. Turner pulled the blank sheet of paper out of the envelope, inspecting it carefully. "Nothing visible, but . . ."

"Don't you find it curious," Agatha said with a wink, "that the victim planned to hand you a blank sheet of paper in an envelope . . . with a stamp?"

Ms. Turner had already started to peel off the postage stamp. Sure enough, there was a microchip hidden underneath it, no thicker than a piece of paper.

LILIAN

Agatha turned to the others. "I think we ought to respect Bismarck's last wishes. Even if you're all spies, you've conducted your business within the law. Lilian Turner won the auction fair and square . . . she should get the information."

Herbert Miller and Kentaro Takagi traded glances, then nodded reluctantly.

Behind them, Dash exclaimed, "Pablo Navarro, I'm turning you over to the captain of this ship. You're the one responsible for the murder of Hermann Bauer!"

Agatha smiled. It was the fourth time that night that her cousin had repeated the same accusation.

But this time he was right.

Mystery Solved...

It was just before six o'clock in the morning when the *King Arthur* slipped calmly into the port at Trondheim. The sun shone brightly in a clear sky.

Agent AP36 was recovering from an uncomfortable overnight train trip and a bouncy taxi ride to the docks. As he joined the crowd waiting to board the ship, he noticed a small group disembarking down a separate ramp. The ship's captain was chatting with Agent DM14, followed by a blond girl who looked about twelve, a large gentleman in a tuxedo, and an irritated Siberian cat.

"DM14, what's going on here?" cried AP36, joining the group.

"This young man is truly a budding detective!" crowed the captain. "There was a murder on board the *King Arthur* last night, but your student solved the case and caught a dangerous assassin!"

A pair of security guards disembarked, escorting a Spaniard dressed as a croupier. They led him unceremoniously to a police car parked on the concrete pier.

"An assassin? DM14, please explain!" stammered AP36.

Dash flashed his best secret-agent smile. "Go ahead onto the ship, sir, and make yourself comfortable. I'll file a full report later. For now, I'm on a family vacation!" Dash strolled away, flanked by Agatha, Chandler, and Watson.

Agent AP36 stood stunned, unsure how to respond.

The *King Arthur* was staying in port until evening so tourists could explore Trondheim's historic harbor, cathedral, and folk-art museum. But Edgar Mistery wasn't satisfied with a simple walking tour. He booked a luxurious family-size speedboat and invited Agatha and Dash to sail the crystal clear waters of Trondheim Fjord, the vast, deep waterway that the lovely Norwegian town overlooked.

They left around ten in the morning. The speedboat, under Edgar's expert control, zipped

along under a brilliant blue summer sky. When they reached the middle of the fjord, he turned off the engine so they could relax in the idyllic surroundings.

Chandler, who'd brought everything they needed, began passing out open-face *smørbrød* sandwiches. Kristi played with little Ilse. Edgar decided to take a dip in the freezing arctic waters to prove his courage and physical strength. He emerged thumping his chest like Tarzan, though his skin looked a bit blue and his teeth chattered.

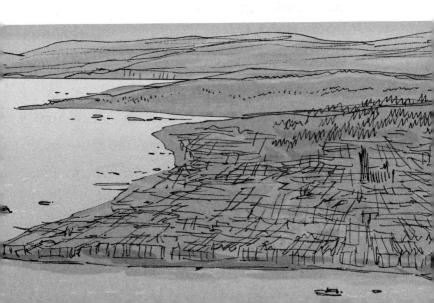

Agatha sat at the bow of the speedboat, writing in her notebook. Watson, curled up on her lap, watched hungrily as marine birds dived into the water, emerging with shimmering, silvery fish in their claws.

Exhausted from lack of sleep and from the previous night's excitement, Dash fell asleep almost immediately under the warm summer sun.

"You look like you're ninety years old," teased his father, ruffling his hair. "Come on, get up. I've got a new challenge for you!"

"Ugh, Dad," grumbled Dash, covering his face with his hands. "Can't you just leave me alone? I just want to rest for a while!"

"Forget it," said Edgar, pointing at a small island half a mile away. "Come on, show me your stuff. Take the helm and steer us to that dock, if you can!"

While Edgar restarted the engine, Dash

reached out for the wheel with a yawn, and stepped on the gas.

Gently at first, and then louder and louder, the speedboat roared toward the wooden pier of the tree-covered island.

"Hey, this is fun!" admitted Dash, as the wind ruffled his hair.

EPILOGUE

"Take it easy, guys," Kristi said cheerfully. "Don't scare Ilse!"

"You've got it, son!" exclaimed Edgar. "Now ease up a little. We're almost there!"

But Watson mistook a flicker of light on the boat's shiny floor for a fish of his own, and chose that moment to pounce right between Dash's feet, tripping him. Still gripping the wheel, Dash suddenly swerved. The boat swung sharply and almost flipped over.

"Look out!" shouted Edgar, clutching his head.

But just as the boat was about to crash into the dock, Chandler grabbed the wheel, moved decisively, and turned the bow back toward the sea.

"You and your stupid challenges!" Dash yelled at his father. "I've had it! Give it a rest for a while!"

"You're hopeless," grumbled Edgar Mistery.

"You can't even steer a boat. And you think you're going to be a world-famous detective? Don't make me laugh . . . You need to hone your skills to become an Eye International agent. It's no job for a wimp!"

Grabbing the wheel, Dash's father continued to mutter. "Director of Scotland Yard? Ha! If you keep on like this, it's going to be years before you even solve your first case!"

Agatha and Dash looked at each other with knowing smiles, and Dash gave his cousin a little wink.

Relive where the mysteries began . . .

Agatha

Girl of Mystery

Agatha's First Mystery:
The Curse of the Pharaoh

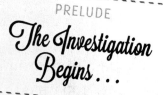

The penthouse sat high atop of Baker Palace, fifteen floors above street level. Its roof was covered with state-of-the-art solar panels, and if you stood on the wraparound terrace and peered in through the tinted-glass windows, the first thing you'd see was a mass of high-tech electronics—monitors, Wi-Fi antennas, and routers—surrounded by pizza boxes, fast-food bags, and dirty socks.

The only person at home was a lanky fourteen-year-old boy, sprawled out snoring on the couch with his dark hair flopped over his face. He had left his seven computers on all night long, downloading data from around the world. His face was lit up by LED lights flashing like fireflies in the darkened room.

Outside the penthouse London, England, was already bathed in a milky haze. It had been a sweltering summer, too hot for tourists, and the Thames River looked like a strip of shiny tar.

Not far from Baker Palace, the famous Big Ben clock tower chimes struck six times. The low notes rattled the walls, but Dashiell Mistery slept like a rock.

Dash was not a morning person. He liked lazing around the penthouse all day and never started his homework till late at night, usually with the music cranked. His report cards said it all: Dash was getting straight As in Surveillance Technologies, but he was flunking everything else.

"Instead of going to that crazy detective school, why don't you study engineering?" his mother would beg on the rare occasions when they had a real conversation. "The Mistery family could use a few people with practical skills." Dash shrugged and said, "Don't forget Grandpa Ellery, Mom. He's at CERN in Geneva studying subatomic particles. That's pretty hard-core." And the conversation would end with his mom sighing, "He's a nuclear physicist, not a normal engineer. All you Mistery men have to do something different!"

Dash secretly liked being known as a "Mistery man." After her divorce, his mother never missed a chance to label the Mistery family a pack of oddballs. First and foremost was her ex-husband, Edgar Allan Mistery, a champion curler. (Curling is an Olympic sport played with brooms and polished rocks on an ice rink; it isn't exactly mainstream.) Every one of Edgar's relatives was part of her roll call of hopeless eccentrics.

6:15 a.m.: Second wake-up attempt. The

words RED ALERT flashed on a monitor screen, accompanied by the theme from *Star Trek*, and a metallic voice that kept repeating, "Man the lifeboats!"

This time around, Dash's forehead was targeted by a laser-tag strobe light. The room looked like the bridge of an alien spaceship.

But it was no use: Dash just rolled over and buried his head in the pillow. Within seconds, he was out like a light.

6:30 a.m.: Final attempt. First the phone rang several times. Then the automatic blinds rolled up, buzzing, while a wall of speakers blasted the latest hit.

A neighbor banged on the door, yelling, "This isn't a nightclub, you slacker!"

Still nothing.

Finally at precisely 6:36 a.m., in the middle of all the deafening chaos, there was a tiny *blip*. It came from a titanium gadget, shaped like a cell phone, which hung from a charger cord over the couch.

That faint *blip* rang in Dash's ears like a volley of gunfire. Without getting up, he reached out, grabbed the gadget, and pressed a few buttons.

A dreadful message flashed onto the screen.

The second that Dash read it, his eyes bulged. "Today?" he yelled. "There's absolutely no way!"

He jumped to his feet. This was a total disaster. He grabbed various remotes, clicking off the alarms, ringtones, and speakers. "There's no time to sort all this out. I have to . . . I have to . . . what do I have to do?!" he exclaimed.

He perched on the arm of a chair, quickly booting up his seven computers, which came to life with a flash of white light. "I'll email Agatha!" he said aloud. "But will she read it in time?" He checked the gadget again, with a grimace. "No, better not. If they hack into my email, it's all over."

Where did he put that cordless phone? He found it under a burger wrapper. Feverishly he scrolled through his contacts, "Adam, Adrian . . . Agatha! Got it!"

He started to text her, but stopped. What if they'd put a bug on his phone? They were experts at stuff like that!

"Okay, don't panic, Dash," he whispered. "Concentrate. What's the best way to get a message to Agatha without anyone listening in?" He ran a hand through his floppy hair and made a decision.

Dash stepped onto the terrace, unlatched the door to his aviary, and grabbed his trusty carrier pigeon. "Time to put you to work, buddy. The Mistery Cousins need you!"

CHAPTER ONE

Those Eccentric Misterys

*A*s the pigeon soared over the suburbs of London, the patchwork of roofs and yards gave way to a wide swath of green: three acres of flowering meadows, fountains, lily ponds, botanical gardens, and quiet, leafy lanes.

Smack in the middle of the park was a Victorian mansion with a lavender roof: the Mistery Estate, home of twelve-year-old Agatha Mistery and her parents.

Agatha was taking a morning stroll in her slippers and bathrobe, dodging the rotating jets of the sprinkler system. The scent of freshly mowed grass tickled her nose—her small, upturned nose, a Mistery family trait.

She carried a cup of steaming tea, which she savored in tiny sips. It was top-quality Shui-Hsien, with a scent like honey and a fruity aftertaste. In a word: superb.

She followed the path to a gazebo, where she sat on a purple swing, resting her teacup next to a pile of letters. Mostly junk mail, bills, and silly postcards from friends on vacation. Agatha didn't bother to read them.

Then she noticed a package on the table. It was covered with stamps, postmarks, and labels from several countries.

What could it be?

"Chandler?" called Agatha.

The Mistery Estate's trusty butler peered out from behind a hydrangea bush, armed with a pair of gardening shears. He was pruning stray twigs, dressed in an extra-large black tuxedo that seemed more suited to a gala event than a garden. An ancient straw hat perched on top of his head.

"Good morning, Miss Agatha." Chandler waved his shears and gave her what passed for a smile, a very faint crack in the great slab of his face. A former professional boxer, he was known for his stony expression.

"What's this?" asked Agatha, picking up the mysterious package. "Where did it come from?"

"From the Andes, Miss Agatha."

"Then it's from Mom and Daddy!"

Agatha crossed her legs and started unwrapping the package, carefully noting the sequence of stamps. "This first one is the postmark of Laguna Negra in Peru," she said aloud. "They're there right now, at thirteen thousand feet above sea level!"

"Just so, Miss."

"And then the post office in Ica, the Andean province," she said, concentrating. "Then Lima, the capital of Peru, then . . . that's strange! Do you see that?"

"Do I see what, Miss Agatha?"

"This stamp, right under the air-mail sticker." Agatha chewed her lip. "It says Mexico City."

Chandler nodded.

"And finally the last stage: from Mexico City to London, endorsed at Heathrow Airport!" She took the last sip of her Shui-Hsien, then pulled her trusty notebook from her pocket and opened it to a blank page. She clicked open her favorite pen, but the ink had gone dry. Frowning, she scribbled a bit, leaving dents in the paper. "Have you got a pen?" she asked Chandler.

Agatha never missed a chance to take notes on an interesting detail. Like every member of the Mistery family, she had her heart set on an eccentric career.

She wanted to be a mystery writer.